To my mother with love
N.W.

MYRIAD BOOKS LIMITED
35 Bishopsthorpe Road, London SE26 4PA

First published in 2005 by
MIJADE PUBLICATIONS
16-18, rue de l'Ouvrage
5000 Namur-Belgium

ISBN 1 84746 113 1
EAN 978 1 84746 113 1

Printed in China

Nadine Walter

Marjolein Pottie

TILLY'S HOLIDAY

MYRIAD BOOKS LIMITED

Tilly the little fly is bored.

"I'd love to take a holiday," she sighed.

Her friends try to persuade her not to go.

"Life isn't easy out there. People don't like flies," they tell her.

"How bad can it be?" Tilly says. "You just need to be friendly!"

She packs a bath towel, a tennis racket
and a pair of big sunglasses in her suitcase.
She looks at her map. "No problem here,"
she says. "The sea is straight ahead."

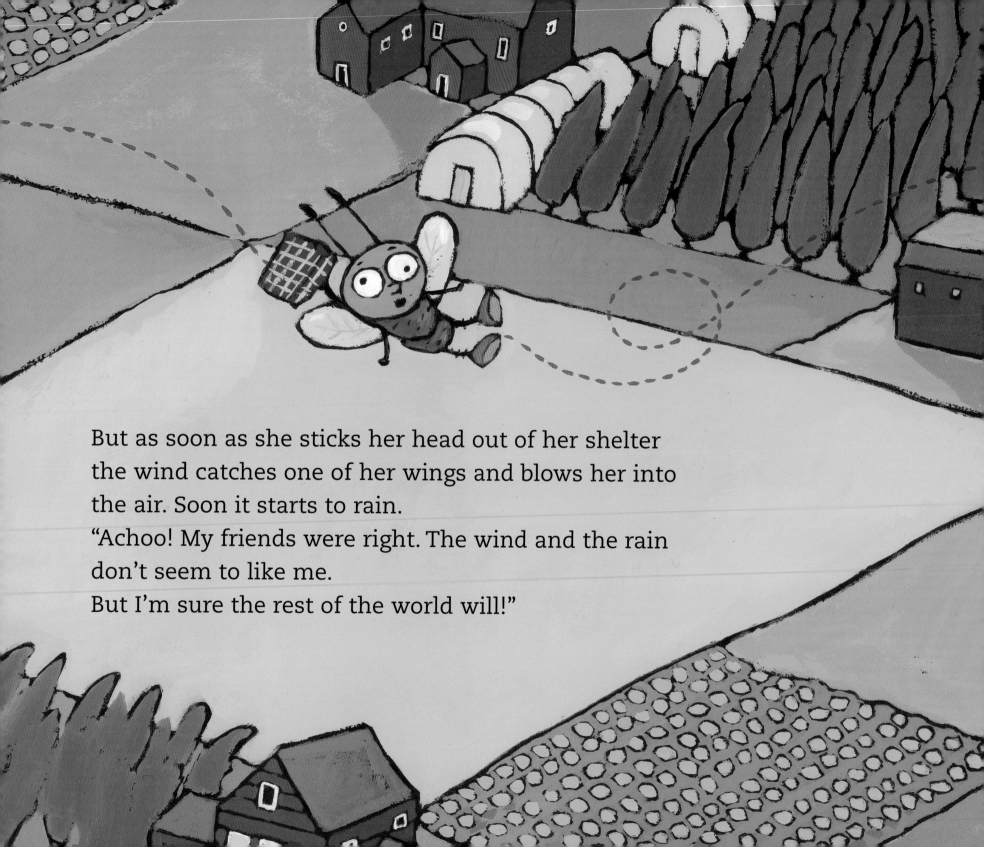

But as soon as she sticks her head out of her shelter
the wind catches one of her wings and blows her into
the air. Soon it starts to rain.
"Achoo! My friends were right. The wind and the rain
don't seem to like me.
But I'm sure the rest of the world will!"

Tilly's wings are heavy with cold raindrops.
And there is no shelter anywhere.
Suddenly she spots a tiny burrow.
"That's just what I need!"
And without hesitation she flies down into it.

"How warm it is in here!
But what's that smell?"
Tilly looks around.
It isn't a burrow.
"It's a cow pat! Ugh!"

Tilly flies up into the rain and soon gets clean again.
She grabs her bath towel and dries herself.
Just at that moment a cow appears. "Hi there, cow!" says Tilly.
The cow flicks her tail and knocks Tilly high into the sky.

"Buzz off, Fly!
I can't stand you!
Get out of here!"

Tilly tries to smile.
"So you don't like me?"

Could her friends really
be right?

Then Tilly hears a noise
and sees a van chugging along
a nearby road.
"Saved at last!" she exclaims.
"I'll ask for a ride and go home
to a warm welcome."

Tilly buzzes in front of the headlights and flaps her wings.
"Hullo, driver. Are you going to town? Can you give me a lift?"
But the driver doesn't see or hear Tilly and the van almost runs her over.

Then Tilly notices
a crack in the driver's window.
She gathers her strength and flies inside.

"Oh it's much warmer in here!"
The driver is a dog with a long nose.
Tilly smiles and lands on it.
"Hullo there! My name is Tilly!"

But the dog snarls, takes off his cap and waves it around.
"Oh no, not another fly," he shouts. "I hate flies.
Get out of my van or I'll swat you to kingdom come."

Trembling, Tilly clings to the dog's cap.
"So, cows don't like my buzzing
and dogs don't like my tickling.
It's not easy being a fly!"

Finally the van slows
down and stops in front
of a house.

Tilly follows the dog into the house.
"How nice and warm it is in this sitting-room!"
she sighs.
But a strange noise attracts her attention.

"Purr, purr, puuuuurr…"
It looks like a warm ball of wool.
Tilly is puzzled and flies over
to take a look.

"Hullo there!" she calls out
in a friendly voice.

The ball of wool suddenly bounces up
and spits at her.
"Hisss! Hissss!" It's a cat!
A big ginger cat with twitching whiskers.

"Oh no!" Tilly says as she
is knocked on to the
sitting room carpet.
"So you don't like me either!"

"Me?" purrs the big cat. "I love you! You are my favourite toy!"
"I am not a toy," shouts Tilly. "You must take good care of me."
The cat's whiskers twitch. "Take good care of you? Ha ha ha!
That's a good joke!" says the cat. "I'll take care of you by not letting you go!"

Tilly quickly escapes into the kitchen.
"What a pretty light hanging
from the ceiling!" she exclaims.
"The dog won't see me up
there and I'll get dry
and warm."

Tilly puts on her sunglasses
and flies head first up to the yellow lamp.

"Ouch, that's hot! It burns!" Stunned, Tilly falls into the dog's soup.

"Not you again!" shouts the dog. "It's fly-swatter time!"

Quickly Tilly swims to the edge of the bowl,
but the dog is already back. "Where are you, Fly?"
This time Tilly has had enough.
"I'm fed up," she says.
"Nobody likes me – and I wouldn't
even hurt a fly!"

"If you want to fight, Dog, step right up!"
She pulls out her tennis racket and
whacks it against the dog's nose.
But the dog is stronger than Tilly.

He opens the window
and tosses the little fly out.
"Good riddance!
And don't come back!"

Tilly lands in a muddy puddle
in the dark.
Suddenly she hears a voice.
"Hullo! What are you doing here Fly?"
Tilly looks up. A big bumblebee is
hovering over her head.
"Don't rrrremain there in the rrrrain
trrrembling with cold!" he says.

"I have nowhere else to go!"
Tilly answers with a sniffle.
"Well, you can come with me.
I am looking for someone to escort
me to a party. Put that suit on!"

Tilly puts on the red boots. She places the pointed hat on her head.
She grabs a little black mask attached to a stick.
"Where are we going?" she asks.

"You will see," the bumblebee answers in
a mysterious voice.

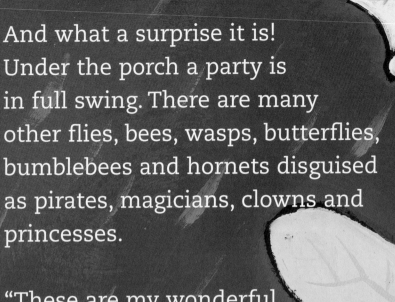

And what a surprise it is!
Under the porch a party is
in full swing. There are many
other flies, bees, wasps, butterflies,
bumblebees and hornets disguised
as pirates, magicians, clowns and
princesses.

"These are my wonderful
friends," the bumblebee
exclaims proudly.

Tilly laughs and dances with joy.
Through the window she can see
the dog eating his soup. He is all
alone, without any friends.
"Too bad. He asked for it. I could
have kept him company but he
chased me away."
Tilly looks around with a happy
heart. She is far better off here.
It is so much fun being
with friends.